To our children, Pablo and Adriana.

First published in the United States of America
in 2014 by Chronicle Books LLC.

Originally published in Spain under the title
Bonjour Camille by BOBO CHOSES in 2011.

Library of Congress Cataloging-in-Publication
Data available.

ISBN: 978-1-4521-2407-0

Manufactured in China.

MIX
Paper from
responsible sources
FSC
www.fsc.org   FSC® C008047

Designed by Laia Aguilar and Lydia Nichols.

10 9 8 7 6 5 4 3 2 1

Chronicle Books LLC
680 Second Street
San Francisco, California 94107

by Felipe Cano
illustrations by Laia Aguilar

chronicle books·san francisco

On Sunday mornings, as soon as the sun comes up, Camille opens her eyes and . . .

puts on her
battledress: a
tutu and a top hat.
She has so many
things to do!

Jumping on the bed until her

nother says, "THAT'S ENOUGH!"

Eating loads and loads of cherries.

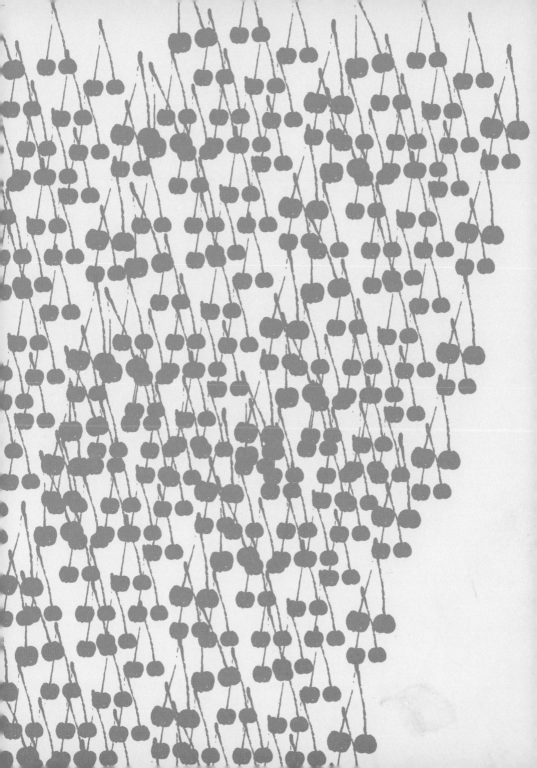

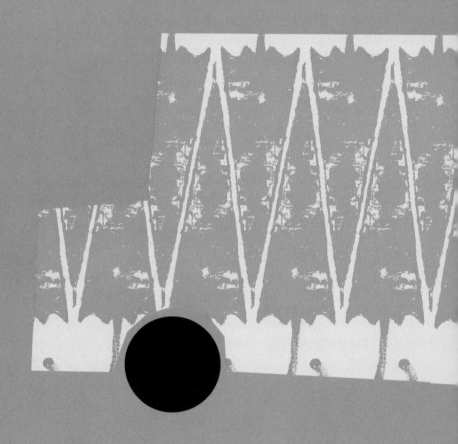

Hiding away all

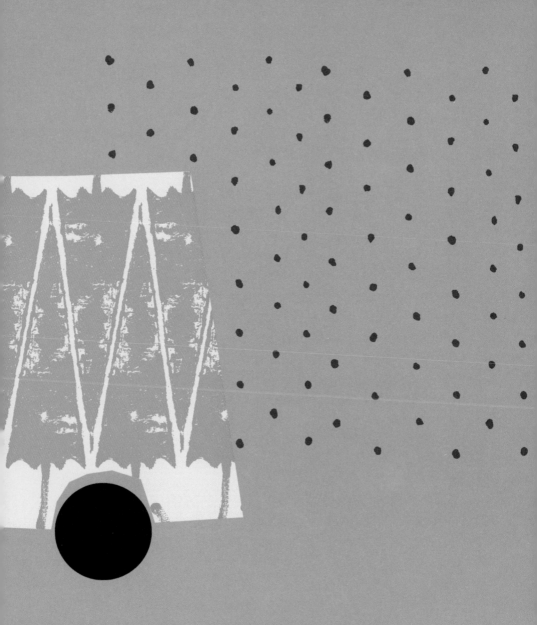

the umbrellas.

Choosing a new favorite color.

CAMILLE

TEO

Giving names to all the waves.

Pablo

Adriana

Louis

isabella

Asking the wind
in a whispering voice
to tell her a story.

Letting an ice cream melt in her hand.

DRAWING THOUSANDS OF FACES ON THOUSANDS OF BALLOONS.

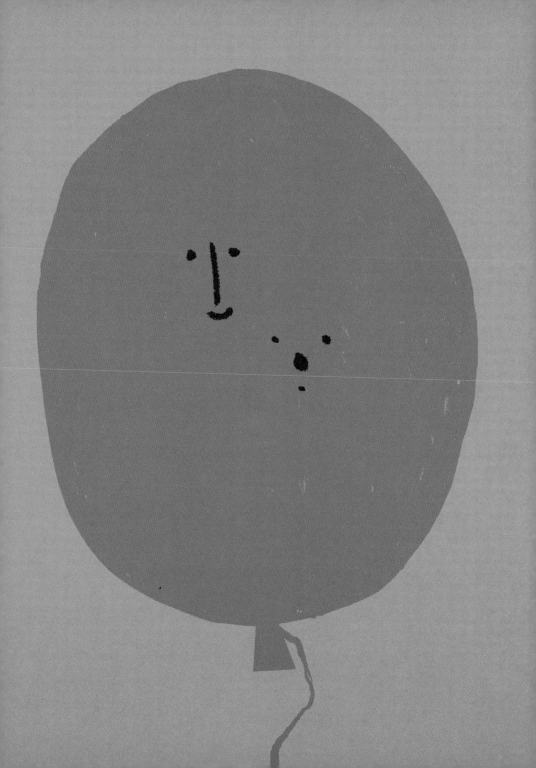

Yelling
at the
winter to
go away.

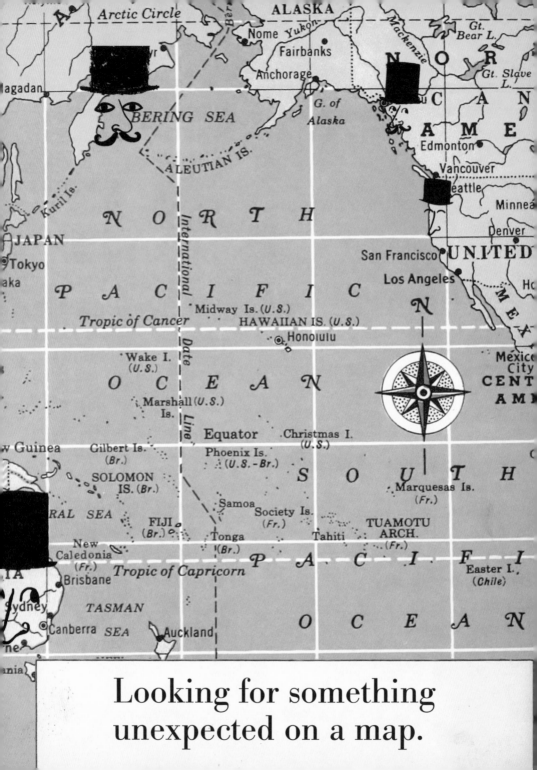

Looking for something unexpected on a map.

Arctic Circle

NORWEGIAN
SEA
ICELAND
Reykjavík
Faeröerne
(Den.)

Str. of Den.

NORWAY
SWEDEN
FINLAND
Oslo
Stockholm
Helsinki
Leningrad
Baltic
Sea
Moscow
R
SO

Julianehaab
C. Farewell

GREAT
BRITAIN
IRELAND
London
Gla
North
Sea
DEN.
BEL.
NE-
GER.
Berlin
POL.
Warsaw
Kharko

Newfoundland
St. John's
C. Race
Montreal
wa
Halifax
Boston
New York
Philadelphia
anta

N O R T H

São Miguel I.
Azores
(Port.)
Sta. Maria I.

Paris
FRANCE
Madrid
PORTUGAL
Lisbon
SPAIN
Rabat
A.U.
ITALY
Rome
Mediterranean
HUN.
YUGO.
RUM.
BUL.
GR.
Istanbul
TURKE
Black
Sea

A T L A N T I C

Tropic of Cancer
Canary Is.
(Sp.)
MOROCCO
(Fr.)
SP. W. AFRICA
Algiers
TUNISIA
(Fr.)
Tripoli
Cairo
ALGERIA
(Fr.)
LIBYA
EGYPT

WEST INDIES
Hispaniol
Caribbean
gota
COL.
a
U.

Cape Verde Is.
(Port.)
Dakar
SIERRA LEONE
(Br.)
LIBERIA
O C E A N
Equator
Amaz
Belém
S
B R A Z I L
BOLIVIA
La Paz
PERU
na
A M   A
fagasta
PAR.
Asunción
Córdoba
URU.
Montevideo
Buenos Aires
ntiago
HILE
ARGENTINA

SAHARA

FR. W. AFRICA
A F R I C A
NIGERIA
(Br.)
GOLD
COAST
Lagos
Natal

ANGLO-
EGYPTIAN
FR.
EQUAT.
AFRICA
SUDAN
ETI

UGANDA
BELG.
Léopoldv
CONGO
AN
KE

Brazzaville
Luanda
ANGOLA
(Port.)
Ascension
(Br.)
St. Helena (Br.)

FED.
OF RH.
& NY.
M

S O U T H

S.W.
Windhoek
AFRICA
Johannesburg
U. OF
SO. AFR.
BECH.
Lou
Mar

Salvador
Rio de Janeiro
São Paulo
Tropic of Capricorn

A T L A N T I C

Capetown
C. of Good Hope

Tristan da Cunha
(Br.)
Gough I.
(Br.)

O C E A N

Pr. Edward Is.
(Br.)

FALKLAND IS.
(Br.)
Arenas
Cape Horn
S. Georgia
(Br.)
Bouvet I.

But then
Camille hears
a voice from the
other side of
the door...

She has so many things to do!

THE END